Summer Snow
on the Mediterranean Sea

Summer Snow
on the Mediterranean Sea

D A R L A   D E S O S A - R O C H A

TATE PUBLISHING
AND ENTERPRISES, LLC

Published by Tate Publishing & Enterprises, LLC
127 E. Trade Center Terrace | Mustang, Oklahoma 73064 USA
1.888.361.9473 | www.tatepublishing.com

Tate Publishing is committed to excellence in the publishing industry. The company reflects the philosophy established by the founders, based on Psalm 68:11,
"The Lord gave the word and great was the company of those who published it."

Book design copyright © 2015 by Tate Publishing, LLC. All rights reserved.
Cover design by Joshua Rafols
Interior design by Gram Telen

Published in the United States of America

ISBN: 978-1-63063-452-0
Fiction / Action & Adventure
15.08.24

To my beautiful niece, Madelyn Elizabeth Hughes, this story is for you. May you always find the magic in your life. I love you.

Love, Aunt Darla

1

Many years ago, when I was just a child, a series of unimaginable events happened to me that, even to this day, I find hard to believe yet they did. The idea of *you* believing it is plausible at best. This is my story, my true story, and so it must be told. I was twelve years old at the time and found myself bored out of my mind, one snowy afternoon.

I was spending the winter holidays with my Grandma Caroline Snow in Cherry Hill, New Jersey. Normally, I would have been thrilled to be there. I loved visiting Grandma Caroline, but this particular day was overcast and blustery, and I was feeling a little melancholy. I was sitting on the puffy window seat, just staring out into the thick lush pine trees that lined Grandma Caroline's backyard. I was daydreaming of dashing up the hill just in front of the trees, with my sled, to go zipping down the rise with the blustery wind in my hair when Tabbey bolted through

the cat door, and my daydream evaporated like cold water droplets on a hot black car in the summer. She jumped up on the window seat next to me with all four paws and brushed her cold multihued fur up next to my leg, arched her back, and purred. She flicked her tail and lied down next to me and looked out the window as peaceful as can be as if to say, "I'm so glad to be inside the warm house!"

I blew a puff of breath on the window. I could see the round spot of fog I'd caused on the glass. The ice crystals where I blew my warm breath melted away in the spot of fog. I ran my hand along Tabbey's bulbous tail as she purred quietly, feeling happier as she was beginning to warm up. Grandma Caroline entered the living room, which was just off the kitchen. She had with her an enormous plate of her famous ice-cold chocolate chip cookies and a tall glass of milk. I knew they were for me. Grandma Caroline always did know how to cheer me up. Her secret was putting the cookies in the refrigerator after they cooled from the oven. The cold fridge made them ice-cold and taste better than anything.

"Summer Elizabeth Snow, what *is* the matter?" Grandma Caroline asked in the kindest voice. She always was so kind and warm.

Looking down at the plate of cookies I was about to devour, I whispered, "I wanted to go sledding today, but it's so cold outside, and the wind is blowing so strong, too strong. Do you think it will stay this cold and windy for my entire visit?" I asked, hoping to hear that it wouldn't, that it would warm up slightly, at least enough for me to sled and make snow angels and a fort. It wasn't asking too much, was it?

"Well, the weather report says it will be a frigid week. I am sorry, Summer," Grandma Caroline answered.

I took a cookie off the tray and chewed it glumly. It was, of course, one of the best-tasting chocolate chip cookies Grandma Caroline had ever made, but I hardly noticed. I was so disappointed about not being able to go sledding and playing in the snow. I had only seen snow a few times and just fell in love with real winter and real snow. I lived in Florida with my mom and dad and only got to see snow when I visited Grandma Caroline in the winter, and so naturally, I thought it was the best thing ever. Mom and Dad thought it would be good for me to get away for the winter holidays and spend some time with Grandma Caroline. Mom hasn't been feeling too well the past few months, and I think they wanted me to visit Grandma Caroline so I wouldn't see Mom feeling so sick and worry.

I drank a long swallow of milk and then put the glass back on the tray that was sitting on the square coffee table. Grandma Caroline's house was always so warm and inviting. She had a large brick fireplace at the far end of the living room. It seemed to reach up the ceiling and was the most perfect fireplace for Santa to come tumbling down with Christmas presents. The fire was lit, and the warmth was so soothing. I loved to sit and watch it and listen to the crackle and snap. The window seat was the perfect place to watch the fire, right next to the window where we sat and the kitchen just on the other side. Grandma Caroline had wallpapered the kitchen in a cheery yellow and silvery white vertical stripe pattern after Grandpa died last year. She said she wanted to change things a little and brighten the house up some. Tabbey stood up and meowed, then took off toward the litter box.

"We could read stories," Grandma Caroline said.

"Yes, I suppose we could," I answered, but not feeling much better about not being able to go outside to play. I wanted to make a snowman too and see if Bobby, the boy who lived next door, wanted to build the fort with me. Grandma Caroline's backyard is quite good for fort building as it is at the bottom of the sledding hill and treed along all the sides. The snowflakes began to hit the window pane just as Grandma Caroline brought over a blanket for me and a crate of storybooks I always loved to read. We sat there for quite awhile, reading all of my favorites—new stories, old stories, and classics, and then Grandma Caroline got up to go into the kitchen. As she stood up from the window seat, her eyes twinkled. She wore a long sleeve turtle neck and a knitted vest over top. Grandma Caroline was such a wonderful person. I just adored her. One could never meet a kinder person or have a better more loving grandmother.

As I continued to read, I began to smell Grandma Caroline's homemade chicken soup simmering on the stove. Grandma Caroline had a special recipe. She used the usual ingredients such as chopped carrots, celery, onions, chicken, and stock, and she added herbs such as thyme and parsley as well. But Grandma Caroline's special chicken soup also calls for special ingredients that she keeps as a trade secret. I knew dinner was drawing near, and much to my chagrin, the snow hadn't let up at all. However disappointed I had been all day, I finally began to cheer up when I saw Grandma Caroline set out her cheesecake on the counter to thaw for dessert. I began to consider that maybe staying inside wasn't so bad after all. Of course, it was getting dark outside, and once morning came again, I'm sure I'd wish for sledding once more. But for now, life was wonderful and blustery, snow or not.

The chicken soup was delicious, of course. The hot and steamy broth filled the whole downstairs with a wonderful scent. Grandma Caroline made the best things to eat. She could have been a world famous chef as far as I was concerned. I could hardly wait for Grandma Caroline to pour her blueberry puree on top of the cheesecake. The flavors melded so well together.

"Grandma Caroline, how did you learn to cook so well?" I asked.

"My grandmother taught me, Summer," she said as she cleared the soup bowls from the round table. I smoothed my hands over the white lace tablecloth and brushed away the crumbs from the bread Grandma Caroline had made to accompany the soup. "You know, she taught me and showed me many things." Her eyes twinkled again as if there were something she wasn't disclosing just yet. Tabbey dashed through the kitchen and round the end of the counter to the bowl of milk Grandma Caroline had just set on the floor. That Tabbey sure had good timing. Grandma Caroline and I giggled at the sight of Tabbey lapping up the creamy goodness.

"Grandma, after dessert, can we dig out all the decorations for the Christmas tree from the attic so when Mr. Whitlock comes to deliver the tree tomorrow, we'll be ready?"

"Sure, honey, where shall we put the tree when it gets here?"

"I think over in the corner of the living room. There's such a big space there, and a Christmas tree would just cheer that corner up."

"That'll be the place then!" Grandma Caroline smiled.

2

We cleaned up the dishes together. I washed, and Grandma Caroline dried. We turned on some Mannheim Steamroller Christmas music, as was our family tradition, and went down the long hallway and up the creaky stairs, just past the bedrooms and headed toward the attic door. The music sounded throughout the home as I yanked the attic door open, and we climbed the stairs. A puff of dust blew into my eyes as the door swung open. Just at the doorway of the attic, there were 5 more stairs to climb. It was quite dark in Grandma Caroline's attic, and I was always a little nervous because it was also so large. On both sides of the stairs were crawl spaces with dusty boxes. There were boxes and crates of all sorts of things once we got to the top of the stairs. Grandma Caroline had a regular storage room set up in the attic. Old lamps and chairs, mannequins from when she sewed dresses, a full-length mirror, and the

Christmas ornaments were all found up there in the attic along with many other objects and boxes and containers. The Christmas ornaments were neatly packed in a large driftwood box Grandpa had made for Grandma Caroline many years ago. The box was so light because of the driftwood, and Grandpa had fashioned little squares inside of it for all the ornaments to fit without breaking.

As I was gathering the garland from the top of the full-length mirror, where Grandma Caroline always kept it so it wouldn't knot together, I noticed a large wooden chest I'd never seen before. It was peculiar because I had been in this attic countless times with Grandma Caroline, yet I've never seen this chest in my life.

"Grandma, is this chest new? It doesn't look new, but I've never seen it before."

It definitely didn't look new at all. As a matter of fact, it looked very ancient. It was rectangular in shape with a raised, curved lid, made of wood, and coated in some sort of shiny shellac in some areas, almost as if some of the shininess had worn off. There were golden carved curlicues and jewels encrusted on it—rubies, emeralds, and diamonds. It almost didn't seem real; it seemed like something out of a storybook.

"Grandma, this looks extremely expensive! Where did you get this? Did Grandpa give it to you?"

"Oh, it's a treasure, a very expensive, cherished treasure for sure, but Grandpa didn't give me that chest. It has been

up here for years, Summer, it's always been up here. You've just never noticed it before. It's interesting that you noticed it tonight, though." Grandma Caroline squinted as if she were thinking.

"Why is that interesting, Grandma?" I ran my fingers through my wavy hair.

"Well, it is interesting that you noticed it at exactly the same age that I noticed it in my grandmother's attic. You see, this chest is very, very old. My grandma had it in her attic too. I had been in *my* grandma's attic many times, just as you have been in this attic many times. I never noticed this chest until I was twelve years old. It was only then that I could see it." Grandma Caroline breathed a sigh of relief. "I was wondering if you were going to see it as I did."

"Grandma, I don't really understand what you're getting at," I said, feeling a bit confused.

"Let me try to explain." Grandma Caroline sat down on one of the old dusty chairs. I sat down in front of her cross-legged on the floor, the gold garland wrapped around my shoulders. I fidgeted with the ends of it in my fingers.

"When I was just your age, I happened to be in *my* grandma Caroline's attic, rummaging through old things she had, just playing and investigating. I never noticed this wooden chest before until that particular visit. And when I opened it and found something I wasn't expecting…" Grandma Caroline stopped and just looked at me. I think she was waiting for me to ask what happened next.

"What was in the chest?" I asked, becoming more interested by the moment.

"Well, I'll get to that. But first, I want to tell you about the chest." Grandma Caroline settled into the chair in such a way that I knew I was in for a long and interesting story. I ran my fingers through my hair once more, feeling more intrigued by the moment.

"I asked my grandma why I'd never seen the chest before, just as you asked me. I was just as interested in how it just suddenly seemed to appear as if it had never been there before. I'd never seen it, so naturally, I assumed it may be new as you did even though it didn't look new. My grandma told me this very story that I'm about to tell you. You see, this chest is very special. Not everyone can see it. Actually, most people cannot see it at all, and the people who can see it, at one point in time, may not always be able to see it. As a matter of fact, I can no longer see it myself." Grandma Caroline looked at me and smiled. She knew I didn't quite understand yet.

"What do you mean you can't see it? It's just right over there behind the mirror," I said and pointed a long index finger toward it.

"Well, I cannot see it anymore. The only thing I see behind that mirror is a bare spot on the floor. This chest chooses to appear to certain people at certain times, and it apparently chooses to appear to these people once they are at least twelve years old. As I told you before, I was twelve when I first saw it, and now, you are twelve, and you've just seen it. Now I don't know everything about this chest, but I do know many things. After I turned about sixteen, I could no longer see it, and I guessed my time with it was over. But I'd say you've probably got a few years to enjoy it and its contents."

"So if it can appear to people and disappear but still be there and I can see it but you can't see it, is it, uh, Grandma Caroline, is it a magic chest?" I asked. Grandma Caroline nodded. "But I thought there was no such thing as magic. Grandma, everyone has always said magic is just make-believe, but now you are telling me it's real?" I was astonished. I couldn't believe my ears, and yet I knew Grandma Caroline would never lie to me or to anyone, but I was having trouble wrapping my mind around the idea that this chest could actually be magic. I just wondered what magic it could do, and I wondered what was inside the chest! *Will this chest grant my every wish? Will it overflow with money? What can it do?* I thought.

"I cannot tell you everything I know, Summer. You will need to learn the majority of the chest's secrets on your own, but I will tell you what's inside of it and what they can do." Grandma Caroline's eyes glimmered with excitement. I knew she couldn't wait for me to delve into the magic of the chest. She was just was excited as I was at the possibilities even though she couldn't see the chest.

"What do you mean *they*? Are there creatures inside, Grandma?" I asked fearfully.

I imagined all sorts of little creatures that could climb out of the chest. The first thing I imagined was the little purplish blue pixies from the *Harry Potter* books. I imagined them flying out of the chest once the lid lifted and causing a wreck in the attic. I then imagined little toy soldiers marching out and starting a hand-to-hand combat war on the attic floor. I imagined little green-haired trolls jumping out and chasing us around. Grandma Caroline chuckled heartily. I thought about all the different adventures I might have. If I could go back in time to a specific culture or period of history, could I also go back in time and slip into a fairy tale too? Or was that just too much magic? I never thought something like this would even be possible in the first place, so the possibility remained at the back of my mind. I wanted to go. I was thrilled and excited, and yet I was scared and confused as well. It was a paradox. It really was.

"No, no, Summer, you silly girl. No creatures, no tiny soldiers, or trolls! Why don't you slide the chest over here though so when you open it, you can tell me what you see, and I can explain *them* to you."

I got up and did as Grandma Caroline instructed and pushed on the left side of the chest. The chest slid across the wooden floor, making a screeching noise to where we were sitting. I knelt down in front of it. Grandma Caroline encouraged me to open the lid. I was excited yet nervous at the same time. I felt a lot of anticipation about what I'd find inside the chest. I lifted the lid all the way until the chest was completely open. It creaked and squeaked, and the joints were stiff, and a puff of dust blew up into my face. I coughed, and I looked down into the chest and found something I wasn't quite expecting.

3

"Well, Summer, what do you see?" Grandma Caroline asked anxiously.

"Grandma, these are all old shoes!" I said, somewhat disappointed. Grandma Caroline leaned back in her chair, tilted her head backward, laughed, and clapped her hands excitedly. I looked up at her, confused once more.

"Oh, Summer, you have no idea what you're in store for!" Grandma Caroline was giggling like a kid in a candy store with a pocketful of change. "All right, Summer, listen carefully. Inside this chest are many pairs of shoes. If you'll notice, there are many different kinds of shoes—old shoes, really old shoes, and slightly newer than old shoes. Do you see?" Grandma Caroline said.

I looked into the chest again, and I did see all sort of funny-looking shoes. Some were covered with dirt; others were polished bright. There were sandals that looked ancient, silk-laced boots, athletic Roman-laced shoes covered in road dust, Chinese Lily Foot shoes, metal shoes that looked like knights wore them, shoes made of leather, Native American moccasins, and wooden shoes. There were just shoes and footwear galore. There were so many different shoes I couldn't find the bottom of the chest. The variety of shoes that were in the chest was just amazing. And it wasn't just that the shoes were so different, but that they were clearly from many different countries and time periods in history. I still didn't understand the magic of the chest, but I was certainly more interested. I always did love it when we learned about historical people and things at school. What I didn't understand was why the shoes were there, what was magical about them, and why there were so many different kinds.

"Ah, so now you see all the many different kinds of shoes in that chest. I don't really know how the magic works, where it came from, or why you and I were chosen to see it, but I do know that it can be wonderful." Grandma Caroline straightened up in the chair. "All right, so now I will tell you about the magic. It's not that the chest itself is magic. It is the shoes themselves that are magic. What you will be able to do is choose the pair of shoes that you like and slip them on. Once you slip them on, you will find yourself in those shoes. You will *literally* be in those shoes. You will magically transport to the place and time of the shoes you choose and go on a mission or adventure in those shoes. When you are ready to end your adventure, all you must do is slip the shoes off again, and you will be home. Do you understand what I'm telling you, Summer?" Grandma Caroline said.

"I think so. So you mean that if I put a pair of shoes on, I will go back to when those shoes were current?" I asked aghast. "And when I want to come home, I just take them off?"

"Yes, dear. This is what I am telling you. However, what is crucial to understand is that both shoes must be taken off to come home. Only slipping off one shoe will not cut it; they both must come off. The shoes in this chest are very special in that they will take you to their time and place as a real person from that time." Grandma Caroline smiled cunningly. "You must also realize that you may look different and act different so that you will fit in to the time and culture of the shoes, but you will have your mind, but you will appear as the person to whom the shoes belong, so be careful and speak slowly."

"Wow, Grandma Caroline, how is this possible?" I asked in wonderment.

I had a difficult time taking in all the information that Grandma Caroline was telling me. I also had the thought at the back of my mind that she was pulling my leg. But this was too big of a story and too long of a story for Grandma Caroline to keep pushing it, if wasn't true. And why would she make it all up in the first place?

I slowly began to wrap my mind around this whole crazy situation as I continued to dig through the shoes in the chest. Grandma Caroline just stared at me with a smile. I wondered if it looked funny seeing me dig through what looked like air to her since she could no longer see the chest.

"Now you may take your first adventure whenever you choose, but I must beg you to be careful as everything is not always as safe as you may think. Danger can lurk in places unexpected. Whilst you are there, you are on your own. Do you hear what I'm saying? I will not be there to help you or protect you. No one will."

I stopped rifling through the box and looked up at Grandma Caroline. "Yes, Grandma, I will be careful no matter what."

"There is one other thing. I explained that you will be transported to another time and place depending upon the shoes you choose to put on, but there is something else I must mention. The time here does not change. No matter how long you are gone, it will be as if a mere moment has passed here. You may be gone for weeks, but no one here will know. This is special because it enables you to go whenever you choose, even if you step away to the bathroom and slip on the shoes, no one will know you've gone." She winked. "I will take the decorations downstairs and set them on the couch so they're ready for the tree tomorrow. You take your time and enjoy looking at the shoes, okay, honey? Make sure you have made a wise decision on which pair of shoes to put on before you do." Grandma Caroline slowly got up from the chair, gathered up the garland from the mirror, and grabbed the box of ornaments. She walked downstairs, and I sat, absorbing all the information she'd given me.

4

I dug down into the chest of shoes and carefully examined the shoes in detail. *Well, I suppose I could take a quick peek into history before bedtime,* I thought. Since Grandma Caroline had explained about the time not being altered here, I figured I could take a quick step somewhere and just have a glimpse before I make my final choice for my big adventure.

I peered into the box about to pick up a pair of shoes when Tabbey bounded up the stairs. She looked at me and tilted her head as if she could also see the chest and was wondering what I was doing rooting through an old chest of shoes. I wondered, *Can animals see the chest too?* "What, you want to come? Sorry, Tabbey, no chance." I scratched her ears and reached back into the chest. I noticed a pair of sandals made of papyrus. I knew that the ancient Egyptians wore sandals made of palm fronds and papyrus, so I knew where I'd be going, if I chose those. I closed my eyes and imagined an olive-skinned woman with flowing white robes and long dark hair standing on the balcony of an white alabaster palace on the shore of the crystal blue Mediterranean Sea. I opened my eyes. I'd always loved Cleopatra and wondered if these sandals would take me to her time and land. Of course, Egyptian sandals could take me to Queen Nefertiti or to King Tut. It could be anyone. Of course, my wish was the elegant Queen Cleopatra. I sighed. It probably wouldn't be her shoes. It would be too good to be true for it to be her shoes.

"Summer!" Grandma Caroline hollered up the stairs. "Your dad is on the phone for you. Come down and say good night, sweetheart."

I laid the papyrus sandals on the pile inside the chest and closed the lid gently. *I'll be back soon*, I thought. "Come along, Tabbey."

I zoomed down the stairs in a race with Tabbey. I got to the bottom of the stairs, and Grandma Caroline handed me the cordless phone as Tabbey swiped her tail across my calf. She turned her head and looked back at me as if to say, *I won, sucker!* "Hi, Dad," I'd said into the receiver. "How's Mom?"

"Hi, honey. Your mom's doing okay. She is resting now, and I think she'll be fine."

"Do the doctor's know what's wrong, Daddy?" I asked, hoping for an answer. Mom had been sick for quite some time. The doctors hadn't been sure what was wrong and were running all sorts of tests. Of course, no one told me much. Being the kid, no one wanted to worry me, but I was worried anyway. I knew more than they realized. I also knew that I was spending this Christmas at Grandma Caroline's so I wouldn't be home while Mom was having all the tests run.

"Well, they're not sure. They are still running tests. Don't worry, promise?"

"Promise," I said with my fingers crossed behind my back.

"All right, well, we better let you and Grandma Caroline get to bed. I love you," Dad said.

"I love you too. Tell Mom too. Here's Grandma Caroline. Bye, Daddy." I handed the phone to Grandma Caroline and went to sit on the window seat again.

I heard Grandma Caroline hang up the phone. She came into the room and sat down next to me. She put her arm around me and whispered that everything would be just fine. "Let's go to bed. We have a big day tomorrow with Mr. Whitlock coming to deliver the tree. You ready?" she asked.

"Yes, I am rather tired now."

We went upstairs, and after I'd brushed my teeth and my hair, Grandma Caroline tucked me in. I had wanted to take a peek into the past with the shoes, but I was worried about Mom, and I thought maybe going to sleep for now was a better idea, and the adventure could be saved for the next day, but I couldn't sleep right away. I wanted to be extremely careful before I made a decision about which pair of shoes I wanted to try on to begin my adventure. To begin with, it was difficult to imagine that this whole thing was real, and that it was *me* to which the chest chose to show itself. I was having a difficult time wrapping my little brain around the entire thing. I also began to think about the adventures that Grandma Caroline might have had. Could she give me some advice about which shoes might be best? I wanted to have the adventure of a lifetime. I also wanted to be safe above all. I had to keep reminding myself that no matter what, I'd be able to come back. No matter what trouble I'd get into, I'd have the chance to get home. All I had to do was to slip both shoes off my feet, and I'd be back in Grandma Caroline's attic amongst the dust bunnies and clutter.

As I lay in bed wide-awake, my mind went back to the Egyptian sandals. I was almost mesmerized with them. I'd always found Egyptian history completely fascinating. I have always been very taken with Cleopatra. I've watched documentaries, read books, looked at pictures and artifacts in museums, and more. But who was she really? I often thought of her as a very misunderstood, passionate mystery. I felt that way about myself often. I never really felt understood by most people I knew. I knew Grandma Caroline understood me, but who else, really? I wondered who really understood Cleopatra. I knew it wasn't her sister Arsinoe. All the conflict within their relationship was tantamount to the eruption of Mount Vesuvius. Was it Julius Caesar? Or Mark Antony? I didn't know. But I felt like I could relate. I felt some sort of draw to her, to the sandals. The funny part was I didn't know if the sandals had anything to do with her or her time period. Of all the people and places in Egypt that the sandals could be related, I had no reason to believe they were connected with her. But I had an inkling deep inside regardless.

That night, I dreamed of many different adventures with the shoes. My dream was a whirlwind of stops along the path of history. I dreamed that I snuck up to the attic in the middle of the night, cracked open the chest, reached in, grabbed a pair of shoes, and shoved them on. I was instantly taken back to a stone castle where I was eyed by a strange boy and a red-haired girl. The boy kept calling the girl Elizabeth. I then shot over to a forest where I was wearing moccasins, and everyone was crying and carrying heavy pouches on their backs. Next, I was riding a horse out in the open plains with high grasses whipping at my bare feet. In the last part of the dream, I was on a train that was packed with people like a can of sardines. People were crying here too, and everyone had a yellow star on their lapels. There was a terrible smell that permeated my nostrils as I woke up with a start and sat directly up in the bed. "Wow, Grandma Caroline was right, some of these adventures could be dangerous," I said to Tabbey that had been sleeping at the foot of my bed until I woke her up with my jolt. "Well, I will just have to be careful where I go, just like Grandma Caroline said." Tabbey put her head back down on her soft downy paws and closed her eyes once more. I settled back down and went back to sleep for what ended up being a restful and sound sleep.

5

The next morning, which was Christmas Eve, I awoke to the sound of Grandma Caroline's voice and a man's voice. At first, I wondered if Daddy had come to tell us Merry Christmas until I realized that he'd still be home with Mom because she was sick. I wondered what was wrong with Mom and why she was so sick. Daddy had said that the doctors weren't sure and were running more tests, and I just had to hope that Mom would pull through and be fine.

I jumped out of bed, brushed my teeth, put my clothes on, and dashed down the stairs to the living room where I found Grandma Caroline and Mr. Whitlock setting up the tree in just the spot I'd wanted. It was such a tall gorgeous tree. Each and every pine needle was glistening from the melted snow, and it smelled ever so sweet of wet spruce in the house. It really felt like Christmastime now with the tree in the house. It also smelled like Grandma Caroline had been making sugar cookies, which of course were my all-time favorite Christmas cookies. Around the holidays, Grandma Caroline made a slew of goodies from chocolate chip cookies to sugar cookies to gingerbread men and fruitcake. Of course, Grandma Caroline's fruitcake was the best, moist and delicious, not hard, heavy, and brick-like like so many fruitcakes were.

After Mr. Whitlock had the tree secure in its holder, Grandma Caroline took the shiny metal watering can and poured some water into the holder for the tree to drink. Grandma Caroline said it was important not to let the tree get too dry. Just then, Tabbey rushed through the kitchen and into the living room. I laughed uncontrollably when I'd seen that Grandma Caroline had tied a little red Santa's hat on her. She looked so adorable and very appropriate as she took her seat underneath the tree.

Grandma Caroline and I spent the morning nibbling on frosted and sprinkled sugar cookies while decorating the tree. We hung all the Christmas bulbs in the old driftwood box that Grandpa had made. We strung the golden garland around the tree and adorned it with multicolored flickering lights. Later, Grandma Caroline got out the stepladder and helped me climb to the top to add the finishing touch—the Christmas angel—at the top of the tree. She said it had been Grandpa's favorite tree topper, and so she'd used it every year.

By then, it was midafternoon, and Grandma Caroline went to lie down and rest on the window seat. Being extremely curious about the chest of shoes, I decided to wander upstairs and take another peak. I gingerly got up from the floor where I was sitting with Tabbey. I glanced at the finished tree and started out of the room when Grandma Caroline opened one eye and said, "I'm sure I don't need to tell you to be careful."

I chuckled. "Grandma Caroline, you know what I'm up to?"

"Don't I always?" She closed her eye once more and seemed to drift off. I padded down the hall and up the stairs until I reached the attic door. I cracked it open, slipped inside, and climbed to the top of the creaky stairs. I knelt down in front of the chest of shoes and cracked open the lid. I looked over all the other shoes with much disinterest. When I spied them, I went right for the Egyptian sandals. I rubbed my fingers over the rough texture. I even smelled them. They smelled like dust—damp and dank. They smelled like they'd been walked on, ran on, and sweated on. I leaned back and sat all the way down with the sandals in my hand. They were just a little bit bigger than my shoes and a bit dusty too. I assumed that they were worn by a young woman because they had a few turquoise beads sewn on the tops of them. The papyrus was braided together to make the shoes. They didn't seem very sturdy as compared to today's standards, but I was looking at a pair of sandals that probably were a few thousand years old.

As I turned the sandals over in my hands, I began to feel a little bit nervous about putting them on and beginning my adventure because I was not sure where exactly in Egypt I would be, who I'd be with, who I'd actually be, and any other detail was also unknown. But an adventure is just that—an adventure. So I decided to take the plunge and slip them on. I took my puffy bunny slippers off and put the right sandal on my foot first. It was a little loose but not bad. I took a deep breath and slowly slipped the left sandal on.

6

I had barely secured the left sandal on my foot when all of a sudden, the room became a blur of attic walls and spinning light. The walls went round and round. Everything in the attic looked as if it were in the same spot, all on top of everything else. It was spinning so fast. I felt the wind being sucked out of me. I heard a loud meow, and I saw a flash of Tabbey's tail fly by, and then suddenly I fell backward and landed on my back right on top of a dusty mound of sand. I sat up and squinted my eyes. The rays from a very bright sun danced upon my face and shone in my eyes. I shook my head, trying to clear it and figure out where I was, and I looked up to see several people standing beside me, none of whom I recognized.

"Charmian, would you please get up? I'm trying to figure out how to get back into my palace, and you're distracting me," one stunningly beautiful woman said.

I climbed to my feet and realized that the sandals were no longer loose. They fit perfectly on my noticeably larger feet. Looking down at myself, I noticed that now I was wearing a flowing white dress, and across my shoulder was a long braid of thick black hair. The woman who spoke to me was simply gorgeous and perfectly refined. She stood tall and erect with her shoulders back. She stood like she was someone important, and she wearing a bright sea blue draping dress that crisscrossed over her shoulders and across her back. It billowed in the light breeze and the heat. Her shoulders were straight and even, and she too had long thick black hair. Her skin was olive-colored, and she wore a golden jewel–encrusted three-quarter-inch tall crown upon her head.

She smelled of honey, and her lips were rose-colored. Her dark brown eyes were lined in black, and she had illustrious long dark lashes. This was no ordinary woman, and the fact that she said she was trying to figure out how to get back into *her* palace, as she'd said, led me to come to only one conclusion. The conclusion that I'd hoped for but only dreamed and wished could be true. This was Queen Cleopatra, queen of the Nile, queen of Egypt, and lover to Julius Caesar and Marc Antony. This was my wish when I looked at those papyrus sandals and slipped them onto my feet. My wish had come true.

7

Cleopatra had called me *Charmian*. I knew that name, and I knew it well. I'd read a lot about Cleopatra, practically everything I could get my hands on, and I knew that Charmian was the name of her most trusted servant and friend whom she'd confide in and whom she could be herself with as rare as that was. As a rich and famous queen, she could not be herself with many people. To think that I had come back as Charmian, well, that was a wish that I couldn't have possibly wished to come true, or even had conceived of. No wonder Grandma Caroline had smiled so big when she'd realized I'd found the chest. She knew what I was in for. I thought that this pair of shoes would have to stay at the top of the chest for future visits. I couldn't imagine taking this adventure and being this close to a queen whom I'd always admired and not coming back.

We stood there in the sand, leaning over a large flat rock. We were contemplating something. Crafting some sort of plan. Cleopatra was a military genius and an all-around genius, come to think of it, so she must have been plotting something important. And here I was, little ole me, a part of it. I glanced at Cleopatra. I was trying not to appear awestruck. I was trying to play the role of Charmian. As the fact is, I could not let it be discovered that I was not who I said I was. She was tapping her long fingernails on the side of the rock, and her thick brow was furrowed. She was concentrating hard.

"I can't believe I have to sneak into my *own* palace. The nerve of my sister Arsinoe to post guards at my palace! Well, there will have to be a remedy for this!" She looked at me. "What do you think?"

Me? She's asking my advice? I thought. I swallowed hard, not knowing quite what to say, but then it hit me. I remembered from the many things I'd read about her that after Cleopatra's father had died, she was coruler of Egypt with her brother. But her sister Arsinoe thought that it should be her who should be queen, not Cleopatra, and that's what led to a civil war where each sister thought they were queen. Cleopatra was basically kicked out of Alexandria and was trying to sneak back in to her palace. Julius Caesar, from Rome, was in the palace, and because Egypt owed so much grain to Rome, Caesar was kind of in charge of the decision of who should be queen. Cleopatra

wanted to meet with him to ensure that he would crown her the rightful queen. After all, she was older than her sister Arsinoe anyway and was the rightful queen. I remembered that Cleopatra was smuggled into her palace wrapped up in a rug. I thought that I could suggest it. After all, it is what actually happened, and she obviously hadn't gotten to that point. And furthermore, I was there for an adventure. I wasn't there to try and rewrite history. "Well, my queen," I began, "you could try and sneak in somehow."

She stared at me, her dark eyes burning into mine. I felt nervous. "And how exactly do you propose I do that?" She stroked her chin with her index finger. Beads of sweat appeared on her forehead.

I just decided to dive right in with the idea. No reason to waste any time. "I suppose," I started slowly, "you could, you know, roll yourself up in a carpet."

She glared at me. "What?" She snapped.

"Well, what I mean is, you could roll yourself up in a carpet and, and send the carpet in to Caesar as a gift." I began shaking my head, feeling more confident. "Once you are inside and Caesar unrolls the carpet to see his gift, you will tumble out and make your case to him. Once Caesar realizes what you've done and listens to what you say, he will protect you. What do you think?" I said shyly.

8

"What do I think?" She snapped again. "I think you are simply *brilliant*, Charmian!" She smiled a cunning smile. A smile kind of like the one I'd always imagined she'd wear.

I stood there, happier and prouder than a peacock to be helping my favorite person from history, the rightful queen of Egypt.

I took in everything I saw, which wasn't much where we were. There was nothing but sand in every direction, except where we were was somewhat of an oasis, of course with sand. We were situated underneath tall palm trees and in a sandy spot with tall grasses. There was a small creek that led from where we were over a sandy hill. I wasn't exactly sure where we were, but I was confident that soon, we'd be back in the palace overlooking the crystal blue Mediterranean Sea. I could just imagine the water glistening in the sun. I couldn't wait to see it.

Sometime later, it began to grow dark and cold. The hot rays of the sun ceased to exist, and in the absence of the heat, the cold stole in like a thief in the night. Two servant men came running up to where we were with a very large Persian carpet. It was elegantly designed with little tassels on the ends. Cleopatra must have sent them to get the carpet. They laid it out flat on the ground.

"Thank you," she whispered as she hugged me. She got down on the ground and lay down flat horizontally on one end of the carpet. It was wide enough for her to lay flat and have neither her feet nor her head stick out on either end. She looked up at me. "Charmian, you will accompany these servants to the palace in Alexandria and explain to Caesar that this is a gift for him from me. Make sure that no one unrolls it until we are in Caesar's presence, and he is watching. I will take care of the rest. Now roll me up."

"How do I know the guards will let us pass?" I asked, feeling a sudden panic and a faultiness in my plan.

"You are resourceful, you will make it happen."

"As you wish, my queen."

Cleopatra looked a bit nervous, and I didn't blame her one bit. I couldn't imagine being rolled up in a heavy Persian carpet. For one thing, it would be beastly hot, and being rolled up in a carpet could easily cause heat stroke, not to mention how difficult it would be to breathe in the tight quarters. It was also probably riddled with bugs and dirt. I did not envy her this task at all. The servants got her rolled up neatly in the carpet and had it tied at each end with ropes. We walked awhile, and the men carried her for what seemed like a very long journey when we finally arrived at the palace.

9

The palace was everything I'd imagined. It sat tall and graceful, very near to the shore of the Mediterranean Sea. Its white alabaster walls shone in the moonlight, and the tall sturdy columns stood strong and royal. I could see the Pharos lighthouse in the distance, out in the glistening sea. I could smell the sea water and feel the mist of sea and salt in the air. I could hear the lapping of the waves hitting the shore. It was dark out, and yet the light from the lighthouse gleamed brightly.

We approach the entrance to the palace and sure enough, guards were standing by. They were tall, muscular, and didn't appear to be weak in anyway. I knew we'd get through but was slightly apprehensive anyway.

We got to the top of the steps, and one of the guards said, "What's this? Who are you?"

"We have been sent by Queen Cleopatra with a gift of a Persian rug for Caesar. Please allow us to pass," I said in a commanding voice, hoping my strong, authoritative tone would convince them. The guards had a short hushed conversation with each other and then moved out of the way of the door and allowed us to pass with a gesture beckoning us forward. I breathed a quiet sigh of relief and led the way with my head held high. I somehow knew where to go even though I hadn't been there before. The fact that I had slipped into the past as Charmian, Cleopatra's main servant, and not just a random person was key. I was her, but she was still her, if that make sense. Her instincts were in charge. I think that is also how I was able to conduct myself in a strong manner.

We headed for Cleopatra's quarters and entered her main workroom. It had a large balcony with heavy red drapes pulled open. There were hand-drawn maps lying on a low marble table, and there were lanterns lit all over the room to provide ample light. Caesar was standing at the balcony window, staring out into the night sea. His back was to us, and I cleared my throat slightly so that he'd know we were there. He spun around to face us. He was dressed in an all-purple toga that was neatly embroidered with gold stitching. This type of toga was called a toga picta, I remembered reading that Julius Caesar wore it. It was worn by kings of long ago, and Caesar thought himself kingly.

"What's this?" he asked.

"This, Caesar, is a gift from Queen Cleopatra," I said and gestured toward the carpet.

"Very well, leave it over there against the wall." He turned to face the sea again. The stars over the sea were very bright, so bright you could almost see their reflection flickering in the waves.

"No, we mustn't leave until it's opened. These are the queen's royal instructions." I panicked. Sweat beaded on my forehead, and my palms also became sweaty. *The carpet must be unrolled; otherwise, Cleopatra may suffocate!* I thought.

Caesar chuckled. "She is a demanding one, isn't she? All right, unroll this gift, this carpet. Let us see the magnificence of it." He lifted his hands, palms up, arms outstretched.

He had no idea what magnificence he was about to see.

10

I nodded to the two servants who laid the rug down gently on the floor, untied the ropes, and stood behind the carpet with their hands gripping the edges. They looked at each other as sweat dripped down their faces and gave a strong pull upward at once, and the rug began to unroll toward Caesar's feet. It was almost like slow motion. The rug was spinning open, and yet it seemed to barely move. Finally, it got to the end, and the last part that covered Cleopatra lifted off, and she tumbled gracefully out and sat neatly on the floor with one knee outward and the other knee pointing upward with her foot flat on the floor. She held her hand up toward Caesar, and with a shocked look on his face, he bent down and took her hand, slowly pulling her to her feet.

"*This* is a *gift!*" he cried.

Cleopatra couldn't have looked more pleased, and she winked at me. She dismissed the servants with a mere look. "Meet me in my quarters later, Charmian. I am once again queen of this palace," she said with utter confidence.

I left immediately and went to the queen's apartments. Cleopatra's main room was more astonishing than I could have ever imagined and more regal than anything described in a book. Her room was gigantic to begin with. She had an extremely large bed, set upon a golden frame with a billowy, silky net around it. This room also had a balcony like in her workroom except this balcony made the other pale in comparison. This was very wide and luxurious, and the view was amazing. The Pharos lighthouse could be seen, and the ships rocked with the rocky waves at the harbor of Good Return. The view went on for miles as if the whole Mediterranean Sea could be seen. On the balcony was a large tub where I assumed the queen bathed in chilled, sweetened milk by moonlight.

I must have been standing there a long time, completely taken with the sights when suddenly, I was snapped out of my awe by the sound of a loud and ferocious growl. I turned to see a multi-spotted African leopard. I froze, jaw dropped at the sight of this great cat. I knew Cleopatra had pet cats but had no idea she had one so large and scary with teeth that could cut steel. I began to back up slowly as the leopard advanced. Its head was down, its teeth bared. I could hear its breathing, heavy and hot. It was so close to

me my legs were pressing against the balcony's half wall as I could see its whiskers twitch, ready for dinner that seemed like it was going to be me.

In that moment of fear, I suddenly heard the sound of a sweet song, a song that Cleopatra was humming as she entered the room. At once, she realized the leopard was about to eat me when she stopped humming and yelled loudly, "Hathor, get out of here! You know this isn't where you're fed! Go on, go!" At once, the leopard turned and scooted out of the room. Apparently, even the great Hathor knew she was the queen.

"Breathe, Charmian, that silly cat is gone." She smirked. I knew by seeing her and the look on her face that she'd convinced Caesar to put her rightfully back in the throne and not Arsinoe.

At that moment, several other servants entered the room, carrying large jugs. They began pouring a white liquid into the tub on the balcony. They poured and poured until the tub was nearly full. Then the last servant to enter brought a large basketful of flower petals and sprinkled them all over the top of the white liquid. Cleopatra, according to what I'd read at school, enjoyed taking baths in chilled, sweetened milk as she believed it made her skin soft and silky. She did have a shimmery glint to her skin. She was very beautiful. She made her way to the tub and pulled her hair up in a tight bun so that it would not get wet. I went back inside her room and got things ready for bed for her. I laid out her nightdress and got ready her perfume wash for her hair.

After Cleopatra's bath, she turned her head upside down over the large white basin in the room. She poured the perfume over her hair and massaged it in. Her skin shone, and her hair smelled of lemon and lavender.

"Tonight was a complete success, thanks to my most trusted friend. Charmian, you were amazing in your thinking tonight. Rolling out of the rug was the most ingenious idea ever," Cleopatra said, very pleased.

"Well, you were the one who convinced Caesar to restore you to the throne, not me," I replied. I sat down on the floor by the lantern as she climbed into her bed.

"Yes, this is true. He liked my moxie. After all, I am Cleopatra VII, my father's daughter. I am rightful ruler of Upper and Lower Egypt. I have the resilience of a wild animal, the gumption of a soldier. I'm resourceful and aggressive. I care about the people. I will lead this country into wealth and success, leaving dust in my path." She closed her eyes and drifted off to sleep. I pulled out the mat underneath the bed and fell asleep myself, praying that Hathor wouldn't come back and have me for a midnight snack.

11

We awoke to the sound of squawking birds and brilliantly bright sunlight entering the room through the large balcony and bathing everything in its warm honey rays. I was the first one up and took the breakfast tray from the servant girl at the door. I cleared Cleopatra's desk and set the tray down. For breakfast, we ate warm bread baked with figs and dates. We dipped the bread in a small dish filled with honey. It was the most delicious bread I'd ever tasted. Of course, it was baked for a queen, so it should have been pretty good. Cleopatra took a long sip of a dark-colored juice in a fancy golden jewel–encrusted goblet. She sat the glass down and peered at me.

"All right. Out with it," she said.

"What do you mean, Your Majesty?" I asked, taken aback slightly.

"There's been something on your mind since yesterday when you fell in the sand. I thought it was just concern for me getting back into my palace. Now I'm back, but you're not. I know you better than anyone, and there is something in your mind. Tell me so I can fix the problem for you." She took another long drink from her goblet.

I stared out the balcony, trying to figure out how to explain about my mom being sick. I was having the best adventure of my life, spending time with my favorite queen from history, and yet I was worried about my mom back home in Florida. I knew she was sick, but I didn't know with what, and I didn't know how to explain that to Cleopatra.

"Well," I began, "I got a scroll from a relative. It said my mother is ill. They don't know with what, but she's very weak and tired. She has no energy at all. I am worried that something worse will happen."

"Is that all?" Cleopatra laughed.

"What do you mean *is that all?*" I was shocked that she'd be so carefree about my mother's health.

"I mean, you silly girl, that I will send Olympos, my personal physician, to see her and make her well. This is not something that the queen cannot take care of for you. You should know this by now, Charmian." She turned to see Hathor trot into the room. I panicked at the sight of the giant African Leopard. Cleopatra could see the fear on my face and directed Hathor out of the room.

I had to come up with a way to tell her she can't send her personal physician to see my mother over two thousand years into the future. She drained the last of the juice from her goblet and ate the last bit of bread before dressing for the day. She dabbed flowery-smelling oil on the insides of both wrists and rubbed it all around her neck and into her hair. She put on a sea green flowing gown with gold threads tied to bunch the sleeves together on her shoulders. She adorned her three-quarter-inch tall jewel-encrusted crown and put her golden arm bracelets and her golden sandals on. I looked down at my own feet and smiled to myself when I saw my own braided papyrus sandals.

I braided my long black hair and changed my white gown and proceeded to explain to Cleopatra about why her personal physician could not go to see my mother. "It's just that I'm not sure where she is. My relative told me in the letter that they moved her to a new house closer to the river so that she'd be more comfortable," I lied. I didn't know what else to say. I couldn't tell the truth. She'd think I'd gone mad. Telling her my mother lived over two thousand years into the future sounded a bit out there.

"All right, Charmian, I will send for Olympos. He can give you a special bag of herbs and spices that I take daily to maintain my beauty and strength. This special blend has been used by pharaohs for years and years. It has been known to heal a variety of ailments. Whatever your mother may have, I believe this will work. When he gathers the ingredients, you can have it sent to your mother." She smiled at me. "After all, it was you who helped me devise that phenomenal plan to take back my palace. This is the least I can do."

I felt like I'd just exhaled an enormous amount of air. I felt like I'd been holding my breath for such a long time. I couldn't believe how easy this had been.

"Let's take my barge for a sail on the Mediterranean. I need to get out and enjoy some fresh salt air." She stood up and made way for the dock and gave the command to ready the queen's royal barge. On her way back to the room, she sent for Olympos.

A short while later, Olympos appeared in the room, standing tall and strong. He waited for her instructions. "Gather together and prepare a bag of my special herbs and spices blend for Charmian's mother, and bring it to me on the ready.

"As you command, my queen," Olympos said and bowed out of the room.

While we waited for the barge to be ready for our sail out on the Mediterranean Sea, I became ever so excited. I felt relieved that I was going to be able to have a bag of Cleopatra's spices. I just knew it would help my mom. Herbs and spices from Cleopatra—from this time and place, from this whole magical experience—I just knew it would help. I just had a feeling about it. Furthermore, I was about to embark on an even more fantastic journey on the

Mediterranean, a sea I'd only ever dreamed of seeing. This trip to Grandma Caroline's house was the best trip ever—finding the chest, traveling back to Egypt and Cleopatra, getting medicine for my mom, and getting to sail though the Mediterranean. Everything was just perfect, what could go wrong?

12

We slipped out of Cleopatra's main room and into the large hallway that lead out of her apartments. We descended the stairs and made our way toward the docks. I heard someone calling to Charmian, realized they meant me, and turned around to see who it was. It was Olympos. He was jogging toward us, yelling for us to wait. He had in his hand a little brown cloth bag. I knew immediately that it was the special herbs and spices Cleopatra had requested for my mother. I graciously took the bag and carefully tied it to the cloth belt on my dress. I was ecstatic to have what I hope would help my mother.

"Thank you, Olympos." Cleopatra squeezed his hand, and he nodded to me, bid us farewell for the afternoon, and turned to go back toward his work area inside the palace.

Cleopatra and I continued to head down to the docks and boarded the queen's royal barge. It was gorgeous, beyond what the books had described. It was made of large wooden planks. It was wide in the middle and narrower toward the tilted upends. The sails were large and brilliant purple. The queen's chair was placed in the middle of the barge with many blue, green, and red pillows, all trimmed in gold stitching. There were white nets hanging down from flat roof just above her seat. The oars were sticking out of the sides of the barge, just at the water level. Many men boarded the barge and went underneath the main floor, and instantly, the barge began to move. As the barge drifted away from the docks, we took our seat. Two large men fanned us with gigantic feathers attached to long wooden dowels. By the seat was a golden tray full of different fruits, from pomegranates to figs to grapes.

We spent the afternoon sunning ourselves on the deck of the barge. It was the most pleasant and awesome afternoon I'd had in my entire life. I lay there, thinking about the chest in Grandma Caroline's attic and how wondrous it was. I wondered where the magic came from but didn't have any idea. Maybe one day, Grandma Caroline could or would explain it to me, or I would somehow find out. Maybe it would be a quest. I didn't know. After relaxing for quite awhile, we began to grow hungry.

"Let us catch some fish to eat," Cleopatra suggested.

I walked over to the edge of the barge and peered down into the water. It was wavy, and the barge rocked back and forth. The water smelled clean and salty, and I could feel the

salt spray on my lips and taste it on my tongue. The water seemed to be very deep where we were, and I could see it glistening in the shine of the midday sun. Just beneath the surface of the crystal sea were fish darting to and fro. There were small fish and big fish, colorful fish and skinny fish, fat fish and long fish, just fish galore.

I was leaning over the edge of the barge, looking at the fish, dazed and transfixed, when all of a sudden, the sound of birds squawked loudly overhead. Still leaning over the edge, I turned my head upward to see the birds, became dizzy, and tumbled into the water. Cleopatra leapt from her seat and dashed to the edge of the barge where I'd been standing.

13

"Help! Get Charmian out of the water now!" she demanded.

Daddy had taught me how to swim. We did live in Florida after all, but the water seemed so deep, and it was so choppy, and I was so dazed. My head slipped underneath the waves, and I reached my arms over my head. I kicked and tried to get back up. My head splashed above the surface.

"He...help me!" I stammered.

I slipped back under and back up again. I could hear Cleopatra, yelling for her servants to get into the water. I heard splashing and commotion. Again, my head slipped under the crashing waves. I tasted saltwater and swallowed some as well. I began to sink deeper and deeper. I was getting dizzy and light-headed from holding my breath. *I'm going to drown!* I thought. *I've traveled back to Ancient Egypt, spent time with Queen Cleopatra, possibly gotten a cure for Mom, and now I'm going to drown in the Mediterranean Sea! I won't be able to tell Grandma Caroline about my adventure or try to save Mom! I can't let this happen. I won't. I guess this is why Grandma Caroline said to be careful.*

Just then, I felt someone tugging at my dress, trying to grab my arms and pull me up, but I was becoming ever more light-headed and dizzy. I wasn't going to take any chances. I grasped the cloth bag of herbs and spices in my hand and reached down to slip my sandals off. I remembered Grandma Caroline telling me that was the way to get back—to slip the shoes off again, both shoes. I was just hoping I wasn't too late. I shoved the left shoe off but blacked out before I could get the right one off.

14

Everything was black. I couldn't see anything. I couldn't hear anything. Then all at once, I began to hear yelling. Someone yelling for Olympos. I opened my eyes to see several people kneeling in front of me. I was on the docks again, in front of the palace. Cleopatra looked frightened. She stroked my hair. Olympos was running down the dock, and he told everyone to back away. He sat me up and slapped me on my back. I coughed up saltwater. I was choking on it. I realized I still had the cloth bag in my hand. I had it gripped tightly in my fist. One sandal was off, and the other was dangling.

"Olympos, is she all right?" Cleopatra demanded.

"Yes, my queen, she needs to cough it out, may be congested for a while, but she'll be fine," Olympos replied. "I will send an herbal tea for her to drink."

Cleopatra breathed a sigh of relief. Two large men picked me up, carried me into the queen's apartments, and laid me down on her bed. Iras, one of Cleopatra's other trusted ladies, came in and helped me into some dry clothes, squeezed my hair to get rid of the excess saltwater, and told me to get some rest. I closed my eyes as Cleopatra entered the room, and just as I was saying good night, Iras slipped the other sandal off my foot.

15

I opened my eyes, and I was lying on the floor in Grandma Caroline's attic. My hair was wet, my clothes were wet, and I was holding a soaked brown cloth bag in my hand. Since I was saved, I hadn't wanted my adventure to end, but at the same time, almost being eaten by an African leopard and nearly drowning in the Mediterranean Sea, I guessed that was enough adventure for one twelve-year-old girl for today. I sat up and rubbed my eyes. I looked over near the chest and saw Tabbey smelling a pair of saltwater-soaked braided papyrus sandals. I leaned over, picked them up, and laid them right on top of the pile of shoes in the chest and closed the lid.

"Come on, Tabbey," I said to the cat. I shuffled, soaked and squishing, downstairs and peaked into the living room at the window seat where Grandma Caroline had taken her nap before I left. I looked at the clock and realized it was only a moment past the time I left this room to head up to the attic. I smiled to myself and headed to my room. I opened up an old wooden jewelry box that was sitting on the dresser and laid my little brown cloth bag of special medicine for Mom in it. I went to the bathroom and took and nice long, hot shower, scrubbing all the saltwater from my skin and hair. After I was finished, I took a little nap myself. After all, I was exhausted from my adventure.

A bit later, I heard Grandma Caroline calling me for dinner. I opened my eyes and realized it was dark, and I smelled Grandma Caroline's famous lasagna. She always made it with fresh Roma tomatoes and lots of cheese, just for me. I dashed down the stairs and sat directly in my seat.

"Well, someone sure looks tired. Want to tell me all about it?" Grandma Caroline smiled.

Over dinner, I told Grandma Caroline everything from the rug Cleopatra was rolled in to the African Leopard to the near-drowning experience in the Mediterranean Sea. Grandma Caroline was so proud that I'd had my first adventure and so excited too. She reminded me again to be careful of danger, though.

"Make sure that no matter what happens, you are able to get those shoes off and get home. Thank goodness you were adored by Cleopatra, and she made sure you got out of the water."

"Grandma Caroline, there's one more thing I want to tell you," I said. "I mentioned to Cleopatra about Mom being sick. She gave me a special blend of herbs and spices for Mom to take. Her personal physician, Olympos, mixed it up and gave it to me."

"Oh, Summer, this is wonderful news! While you were taking your nap, your father called and said that he and your mom were on their way up to spend Christmas day with us tomorrow. He said she's doing worse, and he wanted to make sure that you and she had Christmas together, just in case she didn't make it. The doctors still don't have a diagnosis, so they can't treat her. I just wonder if this blend Olympos gave you will work." She looked at me and smiled. "All we have to do is give it a try, right?" She winked. "Let's bake a special breakfast for Christmas tomorrow and use the herbs and spices, all right?"

"Yes, Grandma, I think that will be just fine." I felt hope and breathed easily.

We spent the rest of the night wrapping presents, eating Christmas cookies, and talking about my adventure. I told Grandma Caroline everything, all about the wonderful things I'd seen, and how beautiful Cleopatra really was.

We went to bed, and I dreamed of salt breezes and sweet pomegranates and figs. I woke to the sound of Mom and Daddy talking with Grandma Caroline in the kitchen. I grabbed the little brown cloth bag out of the jewelry box on the dresser and dashed downstairs. When Grandma Caroline saw me, she scooted them to the living room to sit and wait for breakfast to be ready. Daddy helped Mom

to the window seat where she sat looking utterly exhausted. I hugged them both and wished them a Merry Christmas.

"I'm so glad you're both here," I said.

"Us too," Daddy whispered.

I skipped into the kitchen. "What are we making for breakfast, Grandma?" I asked.

"We're making a pumpkin bread, sweetie." Grandma Caroline winked at me. "Do you have the secret ingredients?"

"Of course," I smiled a toothy smile.

As she mixed the flour, eggs, pumpkin, sugar, and other ingredients in a large metal bowl, she gave me the nod, and I knew it was time to add my herbs and spices to the batter that Olympos had given me. I opened the little bag and poured them into the bowl as Grandma Caroline mixed them in. When it was all mixed, she poured the mixture into a greased pan and put it in the oven to bake.

We went out into the living room and sang Christmas songs to Mom, and before we knew it, the buzzer on the oven went off, and Grandma Caroline and I shot each other a sly grin.

We all went into the kitchen as Grandma Caroline sliced into the hot, steamy pumpkin bread. I could smell the allspice and cinnamon she'd put in the mixture as well as a sweet herbal smell from the herbs and spices in my bag.

Grandma Caroline and I watched hopefully as Mom took her first bite. "Mmm, this is delicious, you two! What a great breakfast bread!" She liked it so much she gobbled it right down. Grandma Caroline, Daddy, and I ate a slice too, but no one enjoyed it quite as much as Mom did.

After breakfast, Mom said she wanted to go and lie down for a while. I felt discouraged. I thought she'd feel better right away. Grandma Caroline saw my face and said, "It's got to digest first. It'll work. I feel it." She winked at me. Her eyes sparkled.

A little while later, while Grandma Caroline, Daddy, and I were sitting in the living room, Mom entered the room and stood in the doorway with the most peculiar look on her face.

"Jean, are you all right?" Daddy asked her.

"Dave, I can't explain this, and I know you'll think this is nonsense, but I've never felt better in my life." She laughed.

Grandma Caroline and I glanced at each other and smiled big. "Thanks, Cleopatra and Olympos," I whispered.

* * *

We never had a better Christmas. I'd gotten what I'd always wanted—a trip back in history and a healthy mom. She was bouncing off the walls.

A few days later, we flew back to Florida, and Mom went to see the doctor again. She explained how she was feeling. They told her they couldn't explain it, but she didn't have any more symptoms. She was well indeed.

I called Grandma Caroline as soon as Mom was finished with the doctor. "Grandma Caroline, it worked. It really, really worked!"

"I knew it would, Summer!" Grandma Caroline laughed.

"I can't wait to come and visit you again on spring break!" I said.

"Me too, and the chest of shoes will be waiting for you," she answered.

I hung up the phone and dashed downstairs. I gathered my beach things because I was going to the beach with Daddy and Mom. And this time, Mom would be bouncing in the waves with us too.